HERBIE DANCES

CHARLOTTE VAN EMST

To Catriona, Fiona and David

A Red Fox Book
Published by Random House Children□s Books
20 Vauxhall Bridge Road, London SW1V 2SA
A division of The Random House Group Ltd
London Melbourne Sydney Auckland
Johannesburg and agencies throughout the world

3 5 7 9 10 8 6 4 2

First published in Great Britain by Hutchinson Children□s Books 1988
Red Fox edition 2000

Printed in Singapore by Tien Wah Press (PTE) Ltd

THE RANDOM HOUSE GROUP Ltd Reg. No. 954009
www.randomhouse.co.uk

Once there was a hippopotamus who loved to dance. His name was Herbie. He lived with his sister, Katie, and every Wednesday afternoon they went to Mrs Flatpaw's ballet class.

'When I grow up,' Herbie would often say to himself, 'I will be a famous dancer. I will leap and twist and turn and jump in all the great theatres of the world.'

Today was Wednesday, and Herbie could hardly wait to get to his class. As the clock struck three he rushed off to find his sister, Katie.

Katie was almost ready. 'Hurry up, or we'll be late!' cried Herbie.

At last they were on their way.

'Good morning, young hippos,' said Minnie Monkey, as they
passed her in the street.

'Good morning,' replied Herbie, politely. 'Can't stop, we'll be late
for our class.'

'How they love their dancing,' said Minnie to Mrs Bear.

'Just in time,' said Mrs Flatpaw, smiling fondly as Herbie and Katie arrived. 'We're going to do something special today.'

'Ready, Class!' she said. 'Today we will learn how to do a big jump called a Grand Jeté.'

Nobody could get it right, except Herbie.

    Mrs Flatpaw tapped her stick. 'Watch Herbie, everyone,' she said.

Herbie leaped beautifully, and everybody gasped.

'Show me,' said Giraffe.
'And me,' said Tiger.

Herbie helped the little ones, too.

The class was a big success, and Mrs Flatpaw said they were all most promising dancers.

The next day, at school, Katie saw a notice pinned on the wall.

It said: GRAND BALLET COMPETITION
                 OPEN TO ALL YOUNG DANCERS OF PROMISE

'That's what we are,' said Katie out loud: promising dancers. Hadn't Mrs Flatpaw said so?

She rushed home in excitement and immediately wrote a letter to enter Herbie and herself.

On the big day, Herbie could hardly wait to tell his friends about the competition. But Ernest Elephant stuck his trunk in the air. 'Ballet is sissy,' he said.

Giorgio Gorilla pulled a face. 'Yeah, ballet's stupid. Ballet is for *girls!*'

'Sissy! Sissy! Sissy!' they cried. Soon the whole class was joining in.
    'Sissy! Sissy! Sissy!' they called after him all the way home.
I can't go in for the competition *now*, thought Herbie, tearfully.
I must hide.

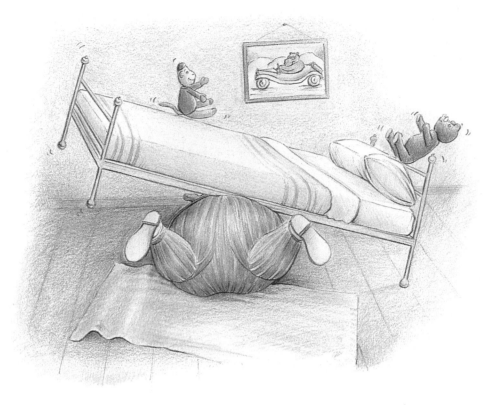

First, Herbie tried squeezing under the bed, but his bottom stuck out.

Then, he hid behind a curtain, but it tickled his toes.

Then, he tried squashing in the wardrobe, but the door wouldn't close.

Last, he tried the bubble bath, but the bubbles got up his nose and made him sneeze.

'I'll just have to pretend to be ill,' he said.

Katie came to see him in bed. She
brought him some medicine
and took his temperature.
'Normal,' she said.
'But I am ill,' insisted Herbie.
'And anyway, I don't like ballet
any more. Ballet is for sissies.'

Katie cried and cried. Big tears rolled down her cheeks as she looked at her lovely ballet dress. Just then, Minnie Monkey looked round the door. Katie told her what had happened.

Minnie marched straight upstairs to Herbie's room. 'Whatever's the matter, young hippo?' she said. 'You *love* dancing.'

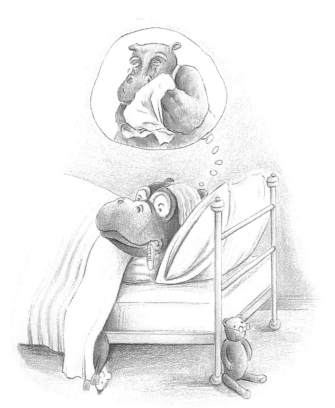

Herbie thought about how high he could jump. He thought about how he could stand on his very tiptoes. And he thought how sad Katie would be to miss the competition.

'I *do* love dancing,' he said. And suddenly he didn't care about Ernest Elephant and Giorgio Gorilla and all the other silly boys in his class. He jumped out of bed, put on his dancing clothes, and ran to find Katie.

'Your medicine has made me better, Katie,' he said. 'Do hurry up or we'll be late for the competition.'

Katie was overjoyed!

In the dressing room all the young dancers were changing.

Herbie and Katie were the last to go on. There was great excitement
as they took the stage.

They danced beautifully.

In the audience, Minnie Monkey wiped a tear from her eye. 'They always loved their dancing,' she said.

Herbie and Katie won first prize: a big golden cup full of silver pennies.

On the way home, they met Giorgio and Ernest.
'Where'd you get that?' they said, jealously looking at
the cup.
　　'We won it,' said Katie.
　　'Yes, ballet dancing,' said Herbie, proudly.

Next day, Herbie took his
cup to school. Teacher
showed the class the
newspaper – there was a
big picture of Herbie and
Katie on the front page.
'Oooo!' said the class.

Afterwards Herbie even let Giorgio hold his cup.

'Perhaps ballet isn't *too* bad,' said Ernest.
   'Show us how you jump,' said Giorgio.
   Herbie showed them. 'If you want to dance properly,' he said . . .

Next Wednesday afternoon, Mrs Flatpaw's class had some new pupils. Everyone enjoyed themselves very much. Giorgio even managed to stand on his toes – well, almost.

'Whoever said ballet was sissy?' said Giorgio, on the way home.
Herbie just smiled, and decided to say nothing at all.